Tuckers' Gold

L. L. Owens

Illustrated by Tim Jones

Rigby

Contents

1 Thoughts of Gold in Independence, Missouri — 1

2 The Big Decision — 6

3 "Jumping Off" from St. Joseph — 11

4 First Crossing — 19

5 Penelope's Travel Diary — 24

6 San Francisco! — 41

7 A Full House — 52

8 The Sun and Moon Chinese Eating Place — 63

9 News from the Diggings — 74

10 An Unexpected Bequest — 80

11 Trouble on Kearny Street! — 89

12 A Job for Uncle James — 95

13 The Rush Is Over — 101

A Snapshot of San Francisco — 106

Thoughts of Gold in Independence, Missouri

December 1848

Twelve-year-old Penelope Tucker entered the living quarters above the family dry goods shop. It was time to help Ma make supper.

As Penelope neared the kitchen, she heard Ma, Uncle James, and Sam, her younger brother, speaking in earnest tones. The moment they noticed her, however, their mouths snapped shut like bear traps.

"What's going on in here?" asked Penelope. She took off her bonnet and smoothed her long auburn hair. "Have I interrupted something?"

Ma and Uncle James traded glances, and Sam blurted out, "We're talking about moving west, Pen! California!"

"*California?*" Penelope exclaimed, her green eyes flashing. "That's on the other side of the continent! It's barely civilized out there!"

"That's not quite true, Penelope," said Uncle James. "People have been settling in California for years. Towns are sprouting up all over the place. Thousands of people are heading to the West."

"And now's the time to go," added Sam. "You've heard all the stories about gold being found in California, haven't you?"

"Yes," Penelope said as she plucked her apron from its peg.

"Well, President Polk made an announcement today. There really *is* gold out there—lots of it! So we might join a caravan and head west to strike it rich!"

"Now slow down, Sam," said Uncle James, ruffling his nephew's sandy-brown hair. "Nobody said anything about getting rich. We want to consider all of our options before we make a final decision. We want to be sure we're doing the right thing."

Uncle James turned to Penelope. Gently, he said, "It's been rough keeping the shop going since your pa died last year. I promised him that I would look after the family, but I never have been the businessman that he was. If the news from the West is true, I could make enough money to take care of all of us. And I would surely like to try.

"Believe me, I know that digging for gold sounds

risky," he continued, "but all the reports say there's plenty of gold—that it's there for the taking. Unfortunately, the only way to 'take' it is to go to California."

Penelope searched Ma's face for answers. "Is it true, Ma? Are we leaving Independence? Are we leaving our home?"

"We may, dear," Ma said seriously. More seriously than Penelope had hoped.

"What about our friends and the shop?" asked Penelope. "And why haven't you said anything before now?"

"As your uncle said, we haven't made a final decision. We had just started discussing the matter today when Sam overheard us. James and I are going to need a few days to talk things through."

Ma paused and touched Penelope's cheek with gentle fingers. "Can you be patient while we do that?"

Penelope sighed. "I'll try, Ma." She wasn't sure that she'd be able to, though. This would be a big change, and she didn't like the sound of it.

"Will you promise to tell us as soon as you decide?" Penelope asked.

Ma smiled and nodded.

Sam shouted, "Let's go digging in the mountains for gold!"

Uncle James winked at Penelope and put a hand on Sam's shoulder. He said, "We have many things to consider, Sam. Don't get your hopes up too high."

After supper, Penelope tried to do some reading by the fire. She found it hard to concentrate, though, so instead she sat quietly and watched Uncle James. He was whittling, as he did nearly every evening.

Penelope often wondered what Uncle James thought about while he whittled. Did he miss the life he had led before Pa died? Did he wish he were back on the road, traveling from town to town, painting portraits and maps, and anything else people paid him to capture on canvas?

Uncle James had given up his own work—his own life, really—to come and take care of the family, and it had not been easy. He didn't know the first thing about running a shop. And although Uncle James would never say so, Penelope suspected that he didn't *want* to know about it, either. Oh, he had tried to learn, but it was easy to see that his heart wasn't in it.

It didn't help matters that a new dry goods shop—much bigger and fancier—had recently opened nearby. It was called Endicott's Fine Dry

Goods. The owner had just moved in from New York. He had 20 years of experience and offered more goods at lower prices. The Tuckers simply couldn't keep up.

Penelope knew that it pained Uncle James to watch his brother's store struggle. Lately, she had seen the strain on his face.

Now she noticed that Uncle James had kept whittling until his twig was nothing but a tiny nub. Things must be worse than I thought, Penelope realized.

She suddenly felt certain that Ma and Uncle James would decide to leave Independence. Their minds were made up, she decided, even if *they* didn't know it yet.

The Big Decision

Penelope and Sam waited impatiently for Uncle James to finish helping Mr. Simpson. As soon as their customer was gone, Ma had said they would close the shop for a little while. "We have some important matters to discuss," she'd told her children.

Mr. Simpson lingered in the shop long after his business was taken care of. He loved to visit and tell stories. Today, he'd brought in a newspaper to show Uncle James.

"My cousin Charlie sent me this from California," said Mr. Simpson. "Look at what people are selling!"

The ad heralded the arrival of a miracle salve that was supposed to attract gold. You rubbed the salve all over your body. Then, the ad promised, as you rolled yourself down the mountain, gold would stick to you. The salve was guaranteed to attract enough gold in one roll to allow a person to live a long and wealthy life!

"What do you do with the gold that's stuck to you?" Sam asked.

"I suppose you scrape it off and put it in a bucket," said Mr. Simpson.

"It sounds like that would sort of hurt," said Sam.

"You bet it would!" Mr. Simpson replied. "You'd never catch me rolling myself down a mountain. Not for any amount of gold! Who's to say I'd be able to stop when I wanted to? Anyway, Sam, this is a great example of lying to the public."

"But it's in the newspaper!" Sam protested.

"Yes, but it's an advertisement, Son," said Uncle James, "not a real news story. It's like the ads we place for the shop—except that we don't make any false claims. The person who wrote this just wants to make money off of people's dreams."

"According to Charlie," added Mr. Simpson, "the ad was real enough to send hundreds of young men to the West."

"So how can you tell what to believe?" Penelope asked.

"That's a good question," said Uncle James. "Sometimes it's hard to know, Penelope. But there's one thing to remember for sure—if it sounds too good to be true, it probably is."

"Well, *I've* always thought the claims of gold in

California are too good to be true," declared Penelope.

"The gold is there," replied Uncle James. "That much we know. You can't get gold without working for it, though."

"True enough," commented Mr. Simpson as he folded his newspaper. Then he said his good-byes, leaving the Tucker family alone at last.

"It sounds to me like you and Ma have made your decision," said Penelope as the door closed behind their customer.

"You're right, dear," said Ma. "We have. Sam, please hang the 'Closed' sign on the front door. We need to sit down and talk."

Sam did as he was told. Then he raced to the back of the store and took a seat. He couldn't wait to get the news. Penelope, on the other hand, *could* wait—forever, as far as she was concerned.

Uncle James got right to the point. "We reached a decision last night. We're selling the shop to Mr. Endicott. He will move our inventory to his store and turn this building into a barbershop. His son will run it. All in all, this is a good deal for Independence, a good deal for the Endicotts, and a good deal for us."

Uncle James paused, but when Penelope and Sam were silent, he continued. "We'll leave from St.

Joseph in April. We can't leave sooner because we need the spring grasses to feed the livestock. St. Joseph is what they call a big 'jumping off' point onto the Oregon-California Trail. We can buy our main supplies there and hook up with the caravan that Sam talked about the other day. A few hundred wagons will make the trip together. We also have an experienced guide to help us along the way."

"Why do we need a guide?" Sam asked. "Can't the caravan follow a trail map on its own?"

"It's not that simple, Sam," Uncle James replied. "The guide provides us with much more than directions to California, although those are important, too. He's familiar with the route, so he knows what we might run into along the way. He can help us avoid some of the problems—or at least deal with them better."

"What types of problems?" Sam asked.

"Well, what if there's a stretch of prairie where there isn't enough grass for the oxen? The guide will know that ahead of time because he's familiar with the trail. He'll be able to tell us where to stop to collect enough grass to make it past that stretch."

Uncle James continued. "The guide knows where to find water, where to get firewood, where to stop and rest—and where *not* to stop and rest. He also has experience fording rivers and guiding wagons through mountain passes. I'm sure that we'll be grateful to have him along."

"You're so quiet, Penelope," Ma said when Uncle James finished. "What are you thinking?"

"I'm not sure, Ma," Penelope answered slowly. "It will take a while for all this to sink in, I suppose."

"I'm sure you'll get used to the idea by April, dear," Ma said. She turned to her son, whose hazel eyes were dancing with excitement.

"Sam?" Ma prompted.

Sam responded by jumping up and down, shouting, "California, here we come!"

Thoughts of the future swirled in Penelope's head as she drifted off to sleep that night. There was a lot to think about, and April would come quickly. Closing the shop . . . saying good-bye to friends . . . traveling across the country . . . making a new life . . . searching for gold.

None of these things had even crossed Penelope's mind before this week. Now she worried and wondered—will we find gold in California? And more importantly—will we survive the long trip to get there?

"Jumping Off" from St. Joseph

April 15, 1849

Penelope woke with a start. She had dozed off in the family's wagon. It took her a moment to reorient herself. She felt the canvas-covered wagon sway as the oxen pulled it slowly along. We're really leaving home, she remembered sadly.

"Welcome back, Pen," joked Sam. "We thought we'd lost you for good."

"Very funny, Sam," said Penelope. "How far did we go while I slept?"

"Look outside," said Ma.

Penelope peered through the canvas flap. They were pulling into a city. Hundreds of wagons—big and small, old and new—lined the streets. Uncle James stopped their wagon near the outfitter's shop.

"We made it to St. Joseph," Uncle James called. "Hop out for a stretch, everyone. I have to go to see about our supplies. We can find the campsite later."

"James, you'll need the list," said Ma. She handed it to Penelope, who jumped down to accompany her uncle.

"Oh, good," said Uncle James. "Would you like to help, Penelope?"

"May I?" asked Penelope. "I'd like to see what people are buying."

"Probably the same things we are," commented Uncle James. "Our guide, Mr. Jackson, sent packing instructions to everyone in the group."

Inside the outfitter's store, a large sign hung over a long counter. It read:

'49ERS—Pick Up Orders Here

☞ **STATE YOUR NAME**
☞ **HOMETOWN**
☞ **TRAVELING PARTY**

NO YELLING, PUSHING, OR FIGHTING

"Looks like we're in the right place," Uncle James said.

"Are we '49ers?" Penelope asked.

"Everyone traveling out West this year is a '49er," replied Uncle James. "And I have a feeling that all of us will look back on 1849 and remember it well."

I'm sure he's right, but I wonder whether our memories will be good or bad? thought Penelope.

The line moved slowly. Many people were leaving for California. A 2,000-mile overland trip was no small matter, after all.

Although she dreaded making this trip, Penelope had to admit that she felt something special in the air. She looked around the store, noticing that the Tucker traveling party was unique. She saw few children close to her and Sam's age. There weren't many women, either—at least not compared to the number of men. Ma had said that many men left their families behind to travel to California. Now Penelope heard several men predicting that they'd find wealth in the gold fields and return home, triumphant, after a year or two. They seemed so sure of themselves!

Although Penelope wished they weren't moving, she was glad that her family had stuck together. It had been difficult enough losing Pa. Now that she was used to having Uncle James around, she didn't think she could bear having him head West without them.

"Next!" shouted the young man behind the counter. Penelope and Uncle James stepped up—

they were finally at the head of the line.

"We're here to pick up the Tucker order," said Uncle James. "That's James Tucker from Independence. We're with the Jackson Expedition, and we jump off from here tomorrow."

"Tucker!" cried the young man to an unseen worker behind him. "James Tucker from Independence! Jackson Expedition!" He turned back and said, "My name is Fred, Mr. Tucker. Let's go over your order to make sure we've got it right."

"Pleased to meet you, Fred," said Uncle James. He nodded to Penelope and she placed the list on the counter.

"How many travelers are in your party?" Fred asked.

"Four," said Uncle James. "Two adults and two children."

Fred looked at Penelope. "Is this one of the children?" he queried.

"Yes," Penelope said. "I'm 12—almost 13. And my brother is 11."

Fred nodded, then made a few check marks and circled some items on the list. He said, "This is right, then. We've outfitted you for four adults, Mr. Tucker. Children their age need the same supplies as the adults.

"So, let's see. For each person, you have 200 pounds of flour, 150 pounds of bacon, 60 pounds of beans and peas, 25 pounds of rice, 10 pounds of coffee, 5 pounds of tea, 20 pounds of sugar, one keg of lard, one keg of clear beef suet, and 10 pounds of salt."

"Goodness, that's a lot to bring!" said Penelope, looking somewhat surprised.

Fred laughed and looked up. "That just covers the necessities, Mr. Tucker. Did you bring other supplies yourself?"

"Yes," Uncle James answered. "We have some cattle and a couple of horses, plus all of our clothes and camping gear, of course."

"Ma packed rice, gingerbread, pickles, vinegar, molasses, citric acid, castor oil, and some dried fruits and vegetables, too," added Penelope.

"Well, I think you're all set," said Fred. "If you pull your wagon around back, my men will load it up." He turned and yelled, "Tucker from Independence! Ready to go!"

Uncle James paid the bill, then reached out

to shake Fred's hand. "Thank you for your help," he said.

"My pleasure, Mr. Tucker," Fred replied. "And good luck. I hope you find the mother lode!"

As they turned to go, Penelope stopped. She was curious about something and wanted to ask Fred while she had the chance. "Will you go out West soon yourself, sir?"

Fred smiled. "Now why would I do something like that, Miss Tucker?"

"For the gold. Don't you want to search for gold, too?"

Fred chuckled. "I've *found* my gold—it's in all these people spending money to outfit themselves for the trip!"

Penelope nodded slowly, puzzling over Fred's words. She would find herself thinking about them often in the coming months.

While Uncle James and Sam saw to loading the wagon, Penelope and Ma talked. Penelope had been thinking about her father a lot. Now she asked, "Ma? Do you think that Pa would have made this trip?"

"I doubt it, dear," her mother replied. "He was so happy in Independence. He loved his work, he loved the shop—and of course, he had all of us."

Ma laughed softly and added, "Then again, I

could be wrong. The news from California has certainly turned more than one man's head!"

"Why do you think Uncle James is so different from Pa?" Penelope asked. "Why does he want to go out West when Pa probably wouldn't have?"

"He's not all that different from your father," Ma said. "James just hasn't found his place in the world yet. He tried doing your pa's job, but that was your *pa's* job—not James's—so it's not surprising that it didn't work out. Everyone needs to find out where they fit.

"The difference between your father and your uncle is that your father didn't need to search for anything. He had what he wanted. He knew where he fit. Uncle James is still searching for that."

That evening, the campsite was buzzing with activity. It's like the annual Independence harvest party, thought Penelope. Except that few people here know each other.

Hundreds of new faces passed by the Tuckers' tent that night. Fires crackled under the clear night sky. Fiddlers played hopeful tunes as people danced. New friends chatted about where they had come from and where they were going. A small cluster of folks standing near Penelope discussed what they would miss most about home.

"I'll miss ice cream," said one woman.

"I'll miss soda water," said a man. "*And* my grandmother's taffy."

"You two aren't thinking clearly!" said another woman.

"What do you mean? What will you miss?" asked the man.

"I'm less worried about missing *sweets* than missing my *sleep*. Can you imagine sleeping in the wagon or on the ground for five whole months? Good-bye, my faithful featherbed! That's what I will truly miss."

Penelope smiled. She was amazed at how many different people had come together to travel across the prairie, over the mountains, and through the desert to the land of gold and promise. And all of them without their featherbeds!

First Crossing

April 16, 1849

Early in the morning, the Jackson Expedition set out for the banks of the Missouri River, where they would make their first crossing. The wagon owners had drawn straws for positions in the wagon train. The Tuckers were lucky to be near the front. "You won't have to eat as much dust there!" joked Mr. Jackson.

The wagons made it to the landing by late morning, but found that they were not alone. Another wagon train was already lined up, waiting to cross.

"Let's ask Uncle James what's going on," Penelope suggested to Sam.

"Don't go far!" warned Ma as the two got out of the wagon.

Soon they were back with some news. "Uncle James says that we should get comfortable," reported Sam.

"We won't be able to cross the river for days!" added Penelope. "The wagons ahead of us go first.

And they have already been waiting for a week because of the rains."

"I had no idea it would be so crowded," Ma remarked. "It's like a busy city street. We had better get settled and make ourselves useful."

"There's nothing much we can do right now, is there?" Sam asked hopefully. Somehow, though, Penelope suspected that Ma would have a different idea.

Ma said, "Sam, I know that you are aching to meet people and learn more about our trip. But there is work to be done. We will be with this group for five months, and you will have plenty of time to mingle."

"What do you want us to do, Ma?" Penelope asked. She wanted to keep busy. It would help to keep her mind off home and what she had left behind.

"I think it's time that we divvied up the chores for the trip. That way we will all know our responsibilities. First things first, though. Let's fix some dinner."

Sam soon called Uncle James back to the wagon, and the family sat down to a simple meal of bacon, cold beans, and coffee.

After dinner, the Tuckers agreed on chore assignments for the journey. Ma would cook, milk the cows, and do the mending. Uncle James would guide the wagon, feed the animals, drive loose stock, hunt, and take his turn with the other men on guard duty. Sam would also guide the wagon and help Uncle James with the animals. Penelope would help with meals, do the washing, and keep the family's journal.

A feeling of restlessness spread through camp that night. People were disappointed by the delay. "Getting to the gold" was on everyone's mind.

"We need to cheer this group up," commented Uncle James as they sat around the fire. In a rich, deep voice, he started singing. Soon men from neighboring tents joined him in long and loud renditions of "The Blue-Tail Fly," "Jim Cracked Corn," and "Buffalo Gals."

In the middle of "Oh! Susanna," Sam stood up to offer a new verse he'd learned in St. Joseph. With more spirit than tune, he sang—

I'll soon be off the trail,
Susanna, don't you fret,
'Cause I'm a '49er,
On my good luck you can bet.
Well, I'm going to San Francisco,
And then I'll look around,
And pick up all those lumps of gold,
A-laying on the ground!

Sam's performance was rewarded with hoots, hollers, and thunderous applause. He grinned, bowed, and swept an imaginary hat from his head.

Then people started trading stories—and dreams—about gold. One man claimed that all Californians kept barrels of gold handy, with flour scoops inside for easy access. Another said that people drank from gold cups and ate with gold forks.

Finally, cheered by music and dreams of the future, the camp settled down for the night.

Five days came and went. At last, it was time to cross the Missouri River.

Spirits had faded during the long wait. But now everyone was bustling about, eager to get on the way. People quickly wrapped tents around poles and stashed them in the wagons. They rounded up their livestock, emptied their coffeepots, and stomped out their fires. They were ready.

The time eventually came for the Tuckers' oxen to pull their wagon across the river. Uncle James guided the team while Penelope, Sam, and Ma watched from the other side. They had crossed earlier in a small ferryboat.

They cheered when the back wheels safely reached solid ground.

As the wagon pulled onto St. Joe Road and followed the deep ruts in the soft earth, Penelope spoke to her mother. "Some people seem sad today, Ma. Have you noticed?"

"I think the trip is finally becoming real to most of us," said Ma. "California is a long way from home."

"Yep," Sam said, "and there's no turning back now. We're on our way."

Her brother's words rang in Penelope's head for the rest of the long, exhausting day. She was on her way out West. And she didn't want to be.

Penelope's Travel Diary

<u>April 21, 1849</u>

It's been five days since we left St. Joseph. We pulled into the Iowa, Sac, and Fox Mission tonight. Uncle James says that the tribes received this land as part of a treaty after they were moved off some other land.

When we arrived, the Indians came by to see if we had trinkets for sale. We didn't have anything for them, but Sam says that Mrs. Crane from a few wagons back sold them her porcelain cups. Mrs. Crane is finding that she packed too many things that aren't meant for rough travel. I'm surprised that those cups made it this far without breaking!

There are a farm and a store and a schoolhouse at the mission. The Reverend and Mrs. Samuel Irvin greeted us. They have run the mission for years. The Irvins had the Indian schoolchildren sing for us. They sang in their own language, so I don't know what the song was about. But it was so beautiful that Ma and I started to cry in the middle of it.

The adults at the mission are learning how to grow corn. The land is filled with rolling hills and groves of trees. I wonder if they have to cut down trees to make room for their crops?

April 23, 1849

We have been going uphill—little by little—since crossing the Missouri. We travel 15 to 20 miles a day. We try to make that distance, anyway. It's hard some days. This trip will take a very long time. I try not to think about it.

Mr. Jackson said that we will be on the trail for at least 150 days, traveling every day but Sunday. Sam asked him why we can't travel Sundays, too, since everybody is so eager to get to California. Mr. Jackson explained that we'll make better time by resting one day a week. The animals need to rest—and so do the people.

We passed Fort Kearny today. Ma says that "Kearny" is the street we'll look for once we get to San Francisco. (That seems so far off!) Mr. Simpson, one of our old customers, arranged for us to stay at his cousin Charlie's boardinghouse there. We are very lucky to have housing already. Ma says that some people don't know what they'll do when they arrive. Of course, men like Uncle James will go straight to the gold fields.

Back to the trail . . . two roads to the West meet here. The sight of endless wagon trains stretching out in all directions is something to behold. When I look at the wagons in the distance, I am struck by how slowly we are moving—especially since I know how far we have to go.

Our oxen pull the wagon at about 2 miles an hour. Earlier, Sam and I watched men on horseback speeding alongside another wagon train. Uncle James said they were probably traveling at 8 miles an hour!

Sam wishes we could make the trip on horseback, but Uncle James told him, "Those men have supplies in wagons just like ours. They can't leave the wagon train behind. And they won't get to California any faster than we do." Still, Sam seems disappointed about our slow pace. I'm not sure how I feel. Every mile we go is another mile from home.

We are camping on the banks of the Platte River tonight. Uncle James has guard duty, so he won't be able to sleep. Black gnats are everywhere and they're making us miserable.

May 4, 1849

We camped near the banks of the North Platte last night. The river flowed near our tents—the sound of it lulled us to sleep.

A frightening scene wakened us at dawn. Sheets of rain and horrible gusts of wind battered our tent. We looked out to see rushing waters—as if we were camped in the river rather than on its banks. I have never seen such a storm!

Men shouted orders, and the camp turned to chaos. The livestock were frightened (as were the humans). Then the storm suddenly passed, leaving a pretty pink sky and remarkably still air. Mr. Jackson told us that we had just experienced the fringe of a tornado!

Sam and I thought of the prairie dogs we see and wondered how they fare in storms. The other day, we saw hundreds of little prairie dog heads popping out of their burrows to watch us roll by. It was the biggest "village" we'd seen so far. This group barked at us, quickly disappeared back into the earth, and then poked their heads up for one last peek. I suppose that they have been kept busy, what with all the wagon trains passing by day after day, month after month.

Tomorrow is my 13th birthday. Ma's making a peach pie for the occasion (from dried peaches, of course!). It feels strange to be celebrating so far from home. I miss Independence and my friends. Things won't be the same in San Francisco.

<u>May 5, 1849</u>

We suddenly find ourselves surrounded by great hills. They aren't mountains, but they are awfully big and imposing. I like them.

We came across the famous Court House Rock today. I think it looks like a giant castle. It's 300 feet high and formed from something called "pipe clay." It's on the top of a ridge of bluffs.

Tonight by the fire, we ate my birthday peach pie and Sam shared the Court House Rock legend with us. (Where does he hear these things?)

According to the legend, Sioux warriors trapped a group of Pawnee on top of the rock. One of the Pawnee prisoners had a vision. In it, he saw a secret trail off the back of the rock. He helped his fellow prisoners escape. Meanwhile, three older Pawnee men volunteered to stay behind. They sang and kept the fires burning to trick the Sioux into thinking they were still trapped on the rock. The plan worked!

The legend says that the old Pawnee men are still there. And that if you camp at Court House Rock, you can hear them singing.

We're camping about 6 miles from the rock. After Sam's story, Ma and I were sure that we heard strange sounds coming from the rock. Uncle James said that it's only the wind, but I like to think it's the Pawnee.

Some from our party decided to walk to Court House Rock tonight. But soon they realized that it only looked like it was nearby. The rock wasn't interesting enough to spend so much time walking at the end of a long day, so they came back.

We all have terrible sunburns. Sam and Uncle James have fared worse than Ma and I have—they are in the sun more than we are. My face stings when I lay my head down. It makes it hard to sleep.

May 15, 1849

We saw Chimney Rock today. A tall tower stands on top of what looks like a large cone.

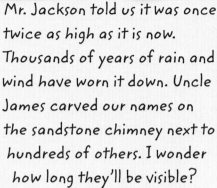

Mr. Jackson told us it was once twice as high as it is now. Thousands of years of rain and wind have worn it down. Uncle James carved our names on the sandstone chimney next to hundreds of others. I wonder how long they'll be visible? Sam has made friends with lots of our fellow travelers. While we set up camp every evening, he tells us the stories he's heard. Last night, he told us about a man who tried to make this trip with just a wheelbarrow. Can you imagine?

May 17, 1849

It's early morning at Scott's Bluff—it's also Sam's 12th birthday. I'll have to remember to tease him about still being shorter than I am.

I usually write in the evenings, but I couldn't sleep. Uncle James is up tending the livestock. The world is quiet, but I can smell coffee, bacon, and pipe smoke from campers already stirring. It won't be long before we're finishing our own breakfast and covering the fire with dirt. Onward!

Every morning, Mr. Jackson rides through the camp and shouts, "Catch up, catch up!" to remind us to get moving. When he thinks someone is moving too slowly, he stops and says, "We will all know who to blame when we're too far behind to make it through the Sierra Nevadas before snowfall!" That usually hurries folks along.

It is breathtaking here. Hills covered with pine trees and cedars surround the valley. Last night, Ma and I went on a long walk to enjoy the scenery. We don't think about it much during the long days. The sunset was so pretty. We hiked up a small hill to see what our party looks like when it circles the wagons for the night. The animals are content to rest and graze in the middle of the circle, and all the travelers seem glad to be sitting by their fires.

Bad news: Uncle James told me that Mr. Smythe's cattle drank from an alkali slough and died in the night. No one knows what Mr. Smythe will do now.

Good news: We made 21 miles yesterday!

<u>May 20, 1849</u>

We are at Fort Laramie! Cheers rang out from the wagons as the adobe walls of the fort came into view. We set up camp 1 mile from the fort. We have been here two days already and will stay one or two more. The livestock need a good rest. There's plenty of grass for them to feed on. Plenty of timber, too. It's a relief to not have to collect buffalo chips for fuel. Sam and I were assigned that chore when we realized that timber was in short supply.

So many people have traveled ahead of us and used things up. One thing's for sure, though: there are always buffalo around to supply us with meat and fuel. That's good, because it takes two or three bushels of chips to make a small fire!

We explored the fort today. The entrance is very small—only one person can crawl through it at a time. Inside, it looks and feels like a small town. There's a sawmill, a public house, and a store. There's even a blacksmith. He is very busy making repairs to wagons!

There's a postal station here, so everyone is writing letters to friends and family back home. I guess some are sending letters ahead to California, too.

May 30, 1849

Our wagon train hit the Sweetwater River and Independence Rock. We're halfway there! We climbed all over the rock before the big celebration tonight. It looks like an enormous bowl turned upside down. It is covered with signatures, dates, hometowns, messages— everyone wants to write or paint something there.

Sam and I signed the rock, too. We decided we didn't want to be the only emigrants in history who didn't. Then we wondered whether we would ever pass this way again. I, of course, hope we do—on our way back <u>home</u>.

The party was so much fun. We danced, played games, sang songs, and ate until we couldn't take another bite. The feast included roast antelope, fried jackrabbit, antelope stew, rabbit potpie, white bread, graham bread, pound cake, jelly cake, peach pie, strawberry pie, custard . . . and more!

Ma looked at my face today and said she'd never seen so many freckles. She says that by the end of the trip, all my freckles will have come together into one big one!

<u>June 3, 1849</u>

We crossed the South Pass today. Mr. Jackson calls it the "backbone" of the Rocky Mountains. It was easy traveling, but even so, we are all tired. Ma thinks it's the change in the air. The temperature did get noticeably cooler throughout the day.

Mr. Jackson warned us that travel from now on will be slower and more difficult. We already know what it's like to trudge through rivers, one toilsome step at a time, with sand up to our knees. The mountain paths will soon become jagged and treacherous.

Sam and I argued today, although I'm not sure why. The trip is wearing us all down. Later, Sam grumbled to Ma that I had the easiest chores to do. Ma never has tolerated much complaining, and she responded by having Sam do the wash this evening. He didn't expect that and was immediately sorry that he'd said anything. He did as he was told, of course.

Sam started talking with one of the men who was washing at the river, too. Sam stopped paying attention and lost a shirt and one of my bonnets in the current.

He apologized to me by offering me one of his

hats. The thought of wearing that dirty old thing made me laugh. I can never stay mad at that brother of mine.

June 4, 1849

We had a frightening day. We pushed on for a while during a heavy downpour. Mr. Jackson had advised us to stop. He said it was too dangerous, but no one would listen. Everyone wants to get to California. Even the idea of a few hours' delay makes people crazy.

Uncle James was walking alongside the wagon. He reached out with a stick to urge on a slow ox. Somehow, he lost his balance and slipped in the mud. He slid under the wagon, and one of the wheels ran over his legs! Sam was out there, thank goodness. He saw what happened and stopped our team.

Ma took off on one of our horses and found Mr. Jackson. He ordered the wagon train to stop for the day; then he helped us. He wouldn't let us move Uncle James until he'd wrapped up his legs.

We were all very worried. Sam asked Ma if we'd have to turn around. Ma said that we'd have to wait and see how badly Uncle James was injured.

That scared me. As much as I'd love to go home, I wouldn't want us to travel as a single wagon.

Uncle James was in a lot of pain. He tried not to show it, but I could tell his legs really hurt.

Mr. Jackson said that Uncle James was lucky. The muddy trail had saved him from two broken legs. (He was kind enough not to mention that the muddy trail he'd warned us about had also caused the accident.) The wagon wheel pressed Uncle James's legs deep into the mud. He is badly bruised, but he'll be fine.

July 11, 1849

We have traveled about 1,200 miles. We stopped at a trading post called Fort Bridger today. There were many Frenchmen and Indians. They trade furs, moccasins, blankets, milk, pantaloons—all types of goods. Milk is much more expensive than at home—10 cents a pint! We saw hundreds of cattle and horses, too.

We rested a few miles from the fort. We knew we'd see Snake Indians on the route. Sure enough, a large group rode up on horseback to greet us. As they approached, a woman placed her baby on a safe patch of land. It was at the bottom of the hill behind our group. She was so frightened of Indians that she didn't want them near her child.

Then another group of Indians rode up behind us and stopped near the baby. From the top of the hill, all you could see were men on horseback. The child had disappeared from view. The woman ran down the hill screaming, "My baby! They've trampled my baby!" When she reached the scene, though, she realized that the men had only formed a protective circle around the child. She nearly fainted!

At the fort, Uncle James found a doctor to examine his legs. They are still purple with bruises, and he's limping some. The doctor said he'd be fine, as long as he didn't strain himself too much.

The rest of us have taken on Uncle James's regular duties. Some "neighbor" men along the train are helping us out, too.

We are definitely continuing the trip.

<u>August 3, 1849</u>

We are following the Humboldt River across Nevada. We hear that the river's nickname is the "Humbug."

We just spent two days at Lassen's Meadow, resting and collecting grasses before we cross the desert. We needed the rest. Our supplies are running low, the animals are tired, and many people have scurvy. Thanks to the dried fruit and citric acid Ma brought along, none of the Tuckers have gotten that disease.

So far, everyone in our caravan has escaped the dreaded cholera. They say it can spread through an entire wagon train in a matter of days. Whenever new groups meet up along the trail, the first question is, "Is there cholera in your party?" We once traveled several miles off the trail to avoid an infected group who'd sent a messenger to warn us.

Earlier, at a fork in the road, we came across a red barrel marked "Post Office." It was filled with notes, mostly for people traveling behind us.

We had a sad day three days back. We met up with fellow emigrants who begged for food. One said, "I have not tasted meat for 20 days." Mr. Jackson said that if we helped them, we would run out of food ourselves. We had to turn them down.

Sam counted more than 100 dead cattle and at least a dozen burned wagons just off the trail that day. Later on, we spotted some men digging graves. It was horrible. Ma and I cried through much of the night.

Talk of the mines is coming up again. It's been a long time since people have been excited about the idea of gold.

We will be in California soon. I hope the days start passing quickly, but Ma says that when you wish too hard for time to speed up, it usually slows down instead. "Time will take its own sweet time," she likes to say.

August 19, 1849

The Forty Mile Desert is as tough to cross as Mr. Jackson predicted. We are traveling over long, hot stretches of dry earth. The land is full of abandoned tents, trunks, wagons, and dead animals. Sam found a few pounds of bacon, but it was spoiled.

People who passed this way before have left behind notes of caution and encouragement. It's comforting to know that people out here are trying to watch out for each other. But, as Uncle James pointed out, we are just as likely to see a poor dead soul stripped of his hat and boots. Ma replied that the poor dead souls understand.

Men with barrels of water approached our expedition this afternoon. They sold us drinks for $1 each—I heard that some people paid $4 and that others along the trail have paid as much as $100! When people are thirsty enough, they will pay anything for water.

<u>August 30, 1849</u>

Our oxen were ready to drop at midday. Their sad, tired heads had hung low all across the desert. Suddenly, though, they perked up. One minute they were refusing to take another step, and the next minute they had their shoulders squared and their noses in the air. I do believe that they walked with more energy than I've ever seen.

Shortly, word spread down the train that water had been spotted on the horizon. It was only 5 more miles to the Carson River.

Uncle James laughed and said, "Those oxen can smell the water!"

Next big stop—San Francisco!

San Francisco!

September 1849

Penelope was relieved to be off the trail. She had always preferred "civilization," as she'd been telling Ma lately.

However, San Francisco didn't seem very civilized to Penelope. It was very different from Independence, Missouri. Some streets were nearly empty; others were filled with rows of tents, food stands, and the occasional wood-framed structure. Most of those were businesses, not homes.

Still, they had reached the West at last. And now they were standing in front of their destination— Charlie Simpson's Boardinghouse.

"We made it!" exclaimed Sam, breaking the silence.

"We did indeed!" said Uncle James. "I was beginning to think this day would never come."

"I wonder what it's like inside," said Ma nervously. She had heard discouraging tales of San Francisco's boardinghouses. Many were little more than hastily built lean-tos in which scores of men crowded each night for a hot meal and an uncomfortable night's sleep on one of the shelf "beds" that lined the walls.

"This looks nice, Ma," said Sam. "Like a regular house."

Ma relaxed. "Yes, it does, Sam," she said. "Shall we knock?"

Penelope eagerly rushed to the front door. As she raised her hand to knock, the door swung open. A family of four came out. They were carrying their belongings and waving to a man standing just inside.

Penelope had never seen anyone like these people before. She was fascinated.

The woman nodded politely. It took a moment for Penelope to realize that the woman was nodding at *her*—and that Penelope had been staring! She had been busy noticing the woman's striking features: dark, almond-shaped eyes, milky fair skin, and gleaming black hair pulled up and wrapped around sticks. She was Chinese, Penelope decided.

When the woman smiled, Penelope blushed in embarrassment. She hadn't meant to be rude. At least the woman didn't seem offended by her staring.

The man at the door called out, "Good luck! Let me know when you're open for business!"

Then his gaze went to Penelope and her family. "Well, hello, young lady," he said. "Are these fine people with you?"

Uncle James scrambled to the door and held out his hand. "My name is James Tucker. Are you Mr. Simpson?"

"That I am. Call me Charlie, please." He looked

at the others and added, "That goes for all of you. I like to keep things simple."

"Thank you, Charlie," said Uncle James. "I believe your cousin in Independence told you to expect us."

"Ah yes, the Tuckers from Independence!" Charlie said. "I understand that you'll head off in search of gold, Mr. Tucker. And the rest of the family will board here. Now, come in, come in."

As she stepped inside, Penelope breathed a sigh of relief. They were in an inviting parlor and the house was spacious and well-furnished. True, it was dustier than Ma might have liked, and there were cobwebs in the corners. Still, she felt at home for the first time in months.

Charlie said, "I should warn you folks that the house is mighty empty right now. And a bit dirty. My helpers quit a few weeks back, I'm afraid. But I've got a nice clean room for you. You're my only boarders, so I could manage that on my own."

"What happened?" asked Uncle James. "I thought every boardinghouse in the city would be full."

"Word got around that I'd rented a room to some foreigners," Charlie replied. "That nice Chinese family stayed here for a few weeks. Some folks didn't like the idea, including the couple that worked for me. So I've had a bit of a dry spell. I don't care, though. They paid for their room and acted real polite. I'll take customers like them any day."

Uncle James helped the family unload their things and settle in. By early afternoon, though, he was ready to leave. Penelope had known all along that her uncle would go straight to the fields. But now it all seemed so sudden.

"Must you go today, Uncle James?" she asked. "Why not start out fresh in the morning?"

"I'm riding with other men from our expedition," he replied. "We'll buy our gear this afternoon, travel this evening, and start work tomorrow morning."

"So soon?" sighed Penelope.

Ma broke in. "Now, dear, this is why we came to California in the first place. We should all encourage James, not try to hold him back."

"Besides," added Sam, "the sooner he gets to the fields, the sooner he strikes it rich! Right, Uncle James?"

"Let's hope that's how it works," said Uncle James.

As he mounted his horse, Ma wiped away a tear. "Be careful, James," she cautioned. "We need you back in one piece!"

"Write often!" said Sam. "I want to hear all about the gold fields."

"Don't forget about us," added Penelope.

"No chance of that happening!" Uncle James exclaimed. "I'll visit as soon as I can. Take care of each other!" With that, he was on his way.

Later, over supper, Charlie tried to raise the family's spirits. "Have you ever heard the story of how gold was discovered in California, children?" he asked.

"Some of it," said Sam.

"But we've heard so many wild stories," added Penelope. "It's hard to know what's true and what's not."

"Well, then, here's the real truth," said Charlie. With obvious enthusiasm, he launched into his tale.

"It all started when Captain John Sutter hired James Marshall to build him a sawmill. One morning, Marshall shut off the water to the mill to inspect the channel. Suddenly he saw something shining in the bottom of the ditch. It was gold. A nugget the size of a pea!

"He told Captain Sutter. The two of them tried to keep the discovery a secret while they figured out what to do. But it's hard to keep news that big from getting out. Soon someone was riding through the streets of San Francisco, shouting, 'Gold! Gold!' and waving a bottle of gold dust in the air. It's been nearly two years now, and people are still rushing to get to the gold fields."

Penelope and Sam hung on every word, imagining the excitement. And now Uncle James was part of it!

Penelope awoke the next morning to the familiar smell of coffee. She yawned and stretched a little, realizing she had slept well.

What's different about today? she wondered. She rubbed her eyes as they adjusted to her surroundings. Then it hit her: the coffee's aroma wasn't mixed with the smell of smoke from a campfire—or the damp, musty earth—or livestock. The hearty fragrance had wafted upstairs from the boardinghouse kitchen into the Tuckers' very own room.

Not only am I in San Francisco, but I slept under a real roof and in a real bed. A feather bed, no less! she thought.

Suddenly, Penelope remembered what the day held. Ma, Sam, and she all needed to look for work. It would be a while before Uncle James could send money back from the fields.

She dressed and hurried downstairs. Everyone else was already in the kitchen. Ma had made herself at home and was cooking up a huge batch of hotcakes and sausages.

"Good morning, Penelope," Ma said. "We're about to eat breakfast. I know you like hotcakes."

"Oh, Ma, this looks wonderful," sighed Penelope. She sat on the bench and helped herself to some fresh fruit. After months of dried apples, it tasted heavenly.

"How did you sleep, Penelope?" asked Charlie.

"Fine, thank you, sir," she answered.

"That's good," he said. "Your brother was up before dawn. I think the fever got to him."

"Fever?" echoed Penelope, looking at Sam with concern.

"Yep," laughed Charlie. "Gold fever. There's a lot of that going around. Your uncle has it. And young Sam shows the signs himself."

"Well, I have the cure," said Ma. "Fresh hotcakes. Who's hungry?"

No one spoke for quite a while after that. At last Charlie put down his fork, sighed, and said, "You were right, Mrs. Tucker. Your hotcakes *are* a cure for the fever. Who'd want to rush off to the gold fields and miss that fine breakfast?"

"Oh, go on," said Ma, blushing.

Charlie's compliment reminded Penelope of his

earlier words. "Tell us more about gold fever, Charlie," she urged.

"Well, there's a real epidemic of it here in San Francisco," Charlie chuckled. "I show all the symptoms myself! Sometimes I dream about closing the boardinghouse and heading for the diggings. Sometimes I just dream about gold, period. And whenever I hear about someone making a big strike, I feel jealous. It's like they're grabbing gold that's meant for me."

"I'm surprised you're still here, Charlie," Penelope said. "After all, Uncle James caught 'the fever' 2,000 miles away. Here you are right next to the gold fields. It's hard to believe there's anyone left in town."

"Well," said Charlie, "not many I know *are* still here. Shops have shut down. Lawyers have left their practices behind. Newspapers have stopped publishing. People leave town every day."

"Is the city getting smaller?" Sam asked.

"You'd think so, with all the people streaming to the fields," said Charlie. "But even more people are coming to town. So San Francisco is growing fast. And that means opportunities for folks like you."

"What sorts of opportunities?" Sam asked. "We all need work—right, Ma?"

Ma glanced at Charlie. Then she said, "It's funny you should mention that, dear. It just so happens that Charlie made a generous offer last night after you children went up to bed."

"What kind of offer?" asked Penelope, looking from her mother to Charlie.

"Charlie needs help with the boardinghouse. And he wants to be able to do some traveling. So he has asked us to work for him. In exchange, we can live here free of charge. The best part, I think, is that we can all work together."

Penelope was stunned. It seemed almost too easy. And it was definitely far better than searching for a job in a strange city she wasn't even sure she liked. She *did* like Charlie's boardinghouse. And Charlie.

"Your ma wanted to know how you children felt about the matter," Charlie said. "So, what do you say? I hope it will be yes. My cousin in Independence speaks highly of all of you. And I could surely use your help."

"It sounds like a terrific idea," Sam said. "Don't you think so, Pen?"

Penelope glanced at Ma's happy face before answering. "It's wonderful. Thank you, Charlie."

Ma relaxed and smiled. Charlie said, "It's settled then. Together, we'll run the best boardinghouse in the whole city."

"Well, then," said Ma, "we'd best get to work, hadn't we? We're going to clean this place from top to bottom!"

Penelope knew by the look in her mother's eyes that they were all going to be busy. Like it or not, her new life in San Francisco had started.

A Full House

Penelope looked around the front parlor. The furniture had been polished and dusted. Every cobweb had been swept away. Firewood was stacked neatly in the corner. Lamps cast a soft glow over the room. It had been a busy few days, but they were ready for boarders.

The boarders were sure to come, too. Charlie had placed a big ad in the *Alta California*. Now Sam held the newspaper and read the ad aloud:

Come One, Come All to

Kearny Street

It's the

Grand Reopening

of

Charlie Simpson's Boardinghouse!

✳Comfortable Rooms!
✳Fair Rates!
✳Full-Service Staff

"When do you think our first boarders will arrive?" asked Penelope when Sam finished.

"Tomorrow, for sure," Charlie said. "We won't have any trouble attracting people. Why, some have come knocking the past few days while we were working. I figure we have room for 12 to 15 men. Besides, I mean what I say in the ad. Simpson's Boardinghouse charges a fair rate. Not like some I know."

"What's a fair rate?" asked Sam.

"There are places that charge as much as five dollars a night—and get it, too. *Everything* in San Francisco costs a lot. But I don't aim to take advantage of people. We can charge half that and still make money."

"That'd be about three hundred dollars a week!" exclaimed Sam, doing the math in his head. "We—I mean, you'll be rich, Charlie!"

"Don't get too excited, Sam," warned Ma. "It'll take plenty of work to earn that money. It will be harder than running the store."

"You've already worked hard," said Charlie with an appreciative look around the room. "Everything looks ready to go. I just need someone to fix that broken fence post out front. Sam, can you take care of that in the morning?"

"No, sir," Sam answered, grinning. "I already fixed it this afternoon!"

"Good work," said Charlie. "I guess that leaves just one thing. I meant to have someone sweep out all the rooms—"

"I did that, Charlie," said Penelope.

"Under the beds?" Charlie asked.

"Under the beds," she confirmed.

"Then I guess we're back in business," Charlie said.

After breakfast the next day, Penelope, Ma, and Sam walked to the marketplace in Portsmouth Square. They had been there twice already. Penelope and Sam were under strict orders to stay away from the square unless they were with Ma. "Anything could happen there," Ma had said.

Penelope had taken that to heart. She felt uneasy anywhere but inside the boardinghouse. She pined for the peaceful and familiar streets of Independence.

The square bustled with activity. Carts, animals, and garbage filled the streets. The sounds of spirited merchants haggling with customers rang through the air. Shopkeepers from all over the world had set up businesses there. So many different languages could be heard that it was almost a surprise to hear English.

After buying supplies for the evening meal, the trio walked over to what would become their favorite shop. It was a brick storefront on the corner of Clay and Montgomery Streets. It offered all sorts of unique and useful things. Today, Penelope and Sam admired a smart Spanish hat while Ma picked out some writing paper and special tea.

When they returned to the house, six dusty, weary-looking men were tying their mules to the fence. Penelope surveyed the group. They're gold miners, she quickly decided. Each wore a slouch hat, a flannel shirt, and sturdy-looking boots—and she saw a pickax strapped to the back of one mule.

"Howdy, ma'am," one of the men said, tipping his hat to Ma. "My name is Buck Johnson. My friends and I heard you were offering beds at $2.50 a night."

"Yes, we are," said Ma with a smile.

Another man, who introduced himself as Rusty, said, "We also heard that you have real beds. Is that true?"

"Sure is," Sam answered proudly. "At Charlie Simpson's Boardinghouse we don't believe in crowding folks together like cattle."

"Come on in," said Ma as she opened the door. "Sam and Penelope, please help these gentlemen with their things."

"No need for that, ma'am," said Buck. "All we have is what's on our backs. We're just in from the fields."

"Did you see our uncle?" Penelope asked excitedly. "His name is James Tucker—from Independence, Missouri. He's tall and thin and he has dark brown hair."

"I can't say that I know him, little lady," chuckled Buck. "There are so many men out there. It's hard to remember who you meet."

"That's enough for now, Penelope," said Ma. "Let's get these men settled." She turned to Buck and the others and added, "Supper is included with your room. We're having beef stew and biscuits this evening, and apple pie for dessert. I hope that's to your liking."

Rusty laughed. "I think you'll find us agreeable to anything you dish up. Just last night, we ate grizzly bear. And not one of us squawked about it!"

"We'll call you when supper is served," Ma said. "Please go on up, choose your beds, and make yourselves comfortable. We sleep three to a room here."

The exhausted miners headed up the stairs. Before long, the sounds of six snoring men drifted down the stairs to the front parlor.

Penelope and James listened as they played a game of checkers during a break from their work. Penelope said, "Can you believe our luck? Six boarders on our first day. I hope business keeps up. Ma really wants us to do a good job for Charlie, and I'd hate to see her disappointed."

"I think we'll do fine," Sam said. "But we can't expect a full house right away. It'll probably take time for folks to hear about us."

A moment later, there was a knock on the door. Penelope and Sam both ran to answer it. Three men stood outside.

"Beds for $2.50 a piece? Is that right?" asked one of the men, as all three walked in.

"Yes, that's right," said Penelope. "Would like to see a room? Each one sleeps three."

"No need to look," the man replied. "We'll take it."

Sam headed upstairs with the men. Soon afterward, Ma glanced into the parlor. "Penelope, did I hear someone at the door?"

"Yes, Ma. Sam is showing three men to their room." As she spoke, there was another knock.

"Three men?" asked Ma. She walked toward the door, saying, "That only leaves us with two vacant rooms. And maybe we have another boarder already!"

By the end of the afternoon, the boardinghouse was full and Ma and Penelope were cooking for a crowd.

Sam banged the supper gong promptly at 7:00. Fifteen hungry men filed downstairs and gobbled up every last morsel of stew, biscuits, and pie. Afterward, they sat at the table with Charlie, drinking coffee and swapping stories.

Penelope and Sam sat nearby, listening. It was all very interesting, but Penelope found herself yawning. As long as the boarders were up, the family was on duty.

Then a strange question from Buck caught her attention. "Who here has 'seen the elephant'?" he asked the group.

Many of the men laughed, and several muttered, "I have!"

"Are there elephants in the gold fields?" Sam asked in a low voice.

"They must be talking about the circus, Sam," said Penelope.

Ma overheard them and smiled. "Actually, 'seeing the elephant' is an expression people use out here. I heard it on the trail."

"I can explain," offered Charlie. He smiled at his audience, happy with his role as storyteller.

"Once there was a farmer who decided to go see the circus. He planned to go to the evening show after selling his vegetables at the market.

"On the way into town, he met up with the circus parade. It was led by a big, beautiful gray elephant. The farmer was so excited. But there was one problem: the trumpeting elephant scared the daylights out of his horses! They bolted and his wagon tipped over. All his vegetables were ruined.

"The farmer said, 'I don't give a hang about the vegetables. I have seen the mighty elephant, and he was worth it!'"

"Since then," Ma added, "people say they've seen the elephant when they mean they've seen it all. Or had the adventure of a lifetime."

"And when someone says it out in the diggings or on the trail," said Rusty, "it usually means that he's ready to give up!"

Several men nodded their heads in agreement.

Apparently they'd had enough searching for gold. Penelope remembered the chores she still had to do after the men went to bed. Wearily she thought, I've had just about enough, too.

The conversation turned more serious as the men discussed their plans. Several were taking a break before choosing another site to dig. Others, like Buck and Rusty, were leaving the fields for good.

"People seem so desperate to *get* here," Penelope said. "Yet you say you're leaving!"

"You can be just as desperate to get out," said Rusty. "Mining is a hard life. Personally, I wish I had never come. I lost my money. And I gave up a whole year of my life—all because I thought I could make a fortune out here."

"Some people *have* made fortunes," said Charlie, his eyes gleaming. "I have a feeling you just need the right technique."

"Well, *I* think it's mostly luck," said Rusty.

"I certainly didn't have much luck myself," exclaimed Buck. "After six months of panning for gold, I have less money to my name than when I first stepped off the boat. I've definitely seen that elephant!"

"Has the gold run out?" Penelope asked. She was beginning to worry about Uncle James. How awful it would be for him—and the whole family— if they had come all this way for nothing.

"No, Penelope, it hasn't run out," Charlie said. "There's still gold to be found out there. I feel it in my bones."

"That's true," Buck admitted. "In fact, I found gold most days."

"Then why do you want to give up?" Penelope pressed. "Isn't looking for gold why you came here?"

"Finding gold was the only thing on my mind when I got here," Buck said with a laugh. "But things have changed."

"How?" Sam asked.

"Well, at first, I figured I'd strike it rich in the gold fields. Now, I have another plan. I want to settle here in San Francisco and have my own shoe shop, like I did back East. There's already one in town, but with all the people flocking here, there ought to be plenty of business. After all, everybody needs shoes. So I intend to strike it rich by providing them!"

Penelope shook her head in confusion. "But after coming all this way, why would you want to go back to the same kind of life you had before?"

"It's *not* the same, Miss Penelope. We're building a new town here, with new people and new ideas."

It was true, Penelope realized. She had seen San Francisco grow and change every day since she had arrived.

"You're right about being able to make your way here as a businessman, Buck," said Charlie. "That's what I'm doing with my boardinghouse. Rooms are in demand. And I like supplying them to people like you."

Then he paused and shook his head slowly. "Still, what I wouldn't give to try my luck in the gold fields!"

The Sun and Moon Chinese Eating Place

October 1849

Penelope sighed. Another knock! Another tired miner or traveler to turn away!

As she walked to the door, she thought back over the past month. Business had been steady—after all, there were more people looking for lodging than there were places for them to stay.

So the Tuckers had been busy keeping things running smoothly. Especially for the last two weeks. Charlie had gone to Sacramento and left them in charge. Penelope was glad he trusted her family with his boardinghouse. Still, without Charlie, there was more work to be done. And she missed his gruff voice and hearty laugh.

"I'm sorry, but we're—" Penelope began automatically as she opened the door. But it wasn't a miner or traveler standing on the other side. It was a beautiful Chinese woman, dressed in robes of red, orange, ivory, and gold. She looked somewhat familiar to Penelope.

Suddenly Penelope realized why the woman seemed familiar. She and her family had been leaving the boardinghouse as the Tuckers had been arriving. "Hello!" she exclaimed. "I saw you on my first day in San Francisco!" Then, a bit flustered, she continued. "Excuse me. My name is Penelope Tucker and this is Simpson's Boardinghouse. May I help you Mrs.—oh my, I don't know your name, do I?"

"Hello, Penelope," answered the woman in perfect English. "Please call me Jing-Li. I remember you, too. Are you enjoying your stay at the boardinghouse?"

"Yes," said Penelope, "but we're not just staying here. My mother, brother, and I are working for Mr. Simpson. Please come in."

Jing-Li entered, and at Penelope's urging, took a seat in the front parlor. Once she was settled, she said, "It is wonderful that you are working for Charlie. I know he needed help. Is he here? I wanted to speak to him."

"I'm afraid not," Penelope replied. "He's out of town right now. Do you want to talk to my mother instead?"

"That will not be necessary, thank you," said Jing-Li. "I simply wanted to tell Charlie that our family's restaurant will open for supper tomorrow. We had hoped that he could be there, but it looks like that is not possible." She rose to her feet saying, "I must be going now. Please tell Charlie we hope to see him soon."

"I know he'll be sorry he missed you," said Penelope. "He thinks a lot of you and your family."

"Thank you for your kind words," Jing-Li said. "Charlie was very good to us, even when it caused trouble for him."

A question that had been burning in Penelope's mind burst out before she could stop it. "Why would people leave the boardinghouse because you were here?" she asked. Then she blushed. "I'm sorry, I shouldn't be asking personal questions. It's just that it seems so unfair to me. I don't understand what the problem was."

Jing-Li lightly tapped the skin on her hand and said, "This was the problem. And this, and this," she added, pointing first to her hair and then to her eyes. "Some people don't want anything to do with the Chinese—or anyone who is different from them. Charlie was not like that, though. It never seemed to occur to him to turn us away. Even when other boarders left. He told us to stay as long as we needed to."

"How terrible for anyone to be treated that

way," said Penelope. "But how wonderful that you met Charlie."

"He became a true friend. We will miss him at our opening." Then Jing-Li smiled shyly and said, "It would be a great honor if you and your family would come in his place."

"We'd love to!" Penelope exclaimed. "Ma is at the market now, but I'll tell her as soon as she returns."

"Wonderful," replied Jing-Li. "We are located on Sacramento Street, or *Tong Yan Gai,* as it is called in our language. We open at 5:00, but you are welcome to arrive early so I can show you around." She went on to give Penelope directions to the restaurant, then took her leave.

When Ma returned from the market, Penelope greeted her with news about the invitation. "May we go, Ma?" Penelope asked.

"It sounds lovely, Penelope," Ma replied. "But I have a house full of hungry men to feed every night."

Penelope's face fell. "Oh, Ma, I'm sorry," she said. "I wasn't thinking. Of course we can't leave the boardinghouse at suppertime. We're too busy then."

Ma smiled. "Wait a minute, dear. You and Sam have been working since we got here. I never could have managed without you. However, I can handle one supper alone, as long as you help me get things ready tomorrow afternoon. So the two of you can go. I am sure Jing-Li will be glad to have as many customers as she can."

Penelope hugged Ma. "Thank you so much! We'll get as much done as possible before we leave," she promised.

Late the next afternoon, Penelope and Sam made their way to the Sun and Moon Chinese Eating Place. It was located in a small, sturdy building. There were even two glass-paned windows in front, a rare find in this city.

Jing-Li ushered the pair inside and introduced them to the rest of the family. "We have a little time before customers begin arriving," she said. "Let me show you around."

The dining area was beautiful. Chinese lanterns were hung around the room and candles flickered on the tables. But Penelope's favorite place was the kitchen. Jing-Li's husband and sons were bustling about, preparing the food. Strange smells filled the air and everything looked exotic and delicious.

"Please sit down," said Jing-Li, pointing to some chairs in the corner. "We will talk until the first customers arrive."

As soon as they were settled, Sam blurted out the

question he asked almost everyone he met. "What made you decide to come to San Francisco?"

"What else?" said Jing-Li. "The gold!"

"Us, too," said Sam. "Our uncle is digging now. Has your husband been to the gold fields?"

"We all have," replied Jing-Li. "We lived in the Chinese camp for a while. It was awful. Especially for the children—it was no place for them, but staying together was important to us. Like many people there, we thought we would find piles of gold to take back to China. But it was difficult."

"Because there wasn't much gold?" asked Penelope.

"Oh no. At first there was a lot of gold to be found. However, it is hard for foreigners to transport gold out of the country. Too many thieves are watching, ready to steal from you. That is what happened to us—our gold was stolen."

"That's terrible!" exclaimed Sam.

"One of my cousins managed better than we did," said Jing-Li with a smile. "He came up with a brilliant plan. He melted down the gold and painted it on his cooking utensils. You could not see the gold—he rubbed soot from the fire on top of it. Nobody bothered my cousin because nobody was interested in stealing pots and pans. He made it back to China safely. When he got there, he melted the gold down again!"

"What about you?" asked Penelope. "Did you come to San Francisco after your gold was stolen?"

"First we went to a different camp. We met some miners who were ready to leave the diggings. They had an old shack that was almost falling down. We bought it from them."

"Why—if it was so awful?" asked Penelope.

Jing-Li laughed softly. "We had a plan. After we bought the shack, we tore up all the floorboards. We knew that those miners had been living there for over a year. So they must have walked in, out, and around it thousands of times. We were able to sweep up piles of gold dust that had fallen off the men's clothes and shoes!"

"So you struck it rich!" cried Sam.

"Yes," Jing-Li concluded. "We used that gold to start this eating place. And now—"

The jingling of the bell at the front door interrupted her. The first customers had arrived! Before long, the dining room was crowded. Most of the customers were Chinese, and the restaurant was filled with excited chatter in a language the Tuckers couldn't understand.

As they ate, Penelope and Sam talked. "It looks like the Sun and Moon Chinese Eating Place is going to do just fine," said Penelope.

"It sure does," agreed Sam.

Then they both fell silent, too busy eating to

waste time on words.

Suddenly, one of the front windows shattered into shards of sharp glass! A rock landed on the floor, not far from Penelope's feet.

"What happened?" she cried, jumping up. She stared at the rock, confused and frightened.

Jing-Li's husband rushed from the kitchen to see what was going on. Jing-Li hurried to see if Penelope had been hurt. Meanwhile, most of the customers sat in shocked silence, staring at the hole in the window. Except for one man, who yanked the door open and went outside.

Penelope quickly assured Jing-Li that she was fine. Then the man who had gone outside to investigate returned. He spoke to Jing-Li in Chinese, shaking his head and waving his arms.

"He could not catch him," Jing-Li translated.

"Who was it?" asked Sam.

"He says it was a young man," replied Jing-Li. "An American, from the wicked words he shouted." She smiled sadly. "I thought *I* was an American now. I thought we all were."

Penelope didn't know what to say. She couldn't imagine why anyone would do such a thing. "Is there anything we can do to help?" she asked.

Jing-Li smiled sadly and said, "Thank you, Penelope. But I see that my sons have already cleaned up the glass. Things are well in hand. Try to forget about this ugliness and enjoy your meal." Then, looking worried, she hurried to check on her other guests.

Back at the boardinghouse, Penelope and Sam told their mother about the rock-throwing incident.

"Why, someone might have been hurt!" Ma exclaimed. "It's frightening. And so unfair to Jing-Li and her family."

"When we left, Jing-Li thanked us for coming. Then she said that we probably shouldn't return. That someone might be angry about Americans going to a Chinese restaurant. Why would anyone think that way, Ma?"

"It's hard to know why some people think as they do," said Ma with a sigh. "But I will tell you one thing. The Tuckers—all of us—will be eating at the Sun and Moon whenever we can."

"You sound like Pa," said Penelope softly. "I remember what he used to say about the unfairness of slavery."

Eyes glistening, Ma changed the subject. "Now tell me about the restaurant—and the food," she said briskly.

Penelope and Sam described everything. How the restaurant looked, what they ate, even Jing-Li's story of finding gold under the floorboards.

"Does Jing-Li accept gold dust as payment?" Ma asked. That was on many merchants' minds these days. Often, shopkeepers had little choice if they wanted to get paid.

"I saw someone pay with gold dust," said Penelope. "But Jing-Li is like us. She would rather get gold coins." She paused, then said, "Ma, did you ever think you'd get so used to dealing with flakes of gold?"

"I hadn't really thought about it, Penelope," said Ma. "Why do you ask?"

"I don't know," said Penelope. "It's just that gold doesn't seem that special to me. It did at first. But now handling it is no different than handling the money we took at the dry goods shop.

"We came here to start a whole new life," she continued. "But it's starting to feel almost like the life we had before. It makes me wonder why we've gone to so much trouble."

"Don't you like it here?" Ma asked.

"I honestly don't know, Ma," said Penelope. "Right now I'm just trying to understand how life has changed and how it has stayed the same."

"I don't know what's the matter with you, Pen," said Sam. "Gold *is* special. And San Francisco is a great place to live. You think too much!"

Penelope laughed. She suspected her brother was right, but that didn't stop the confused thoughts from swirling through her mind.

News from the Diggings

December 1849

Penelope shivered. It was a cold, windy December morning. She and Sam were running errands for Ma, but all she could think about was the warm boardinghouse. She was tired of slogging along the wet, muddy roads. More than a foot of rain had fallen the day before. The streets were still a mess.

"Look at the line!" Sam exclaimed as they approached the post office.

"That's right! It's delivery day," said Penelope. "As long as we're out, we should pick up the mail."

It was an hour later by the time Penelope and Sam reached the window to collect their mail. Eagerly they examined the parcels and letters. Penelope's face lit up when she recognized the handwriting on one letter.

"Sam, this is from Uncle James!" she said. "It's been weeks since we've heard from him."

"And look, Pen," said Sam. "We have one from Charlie, too."

Charlie had been gone for a month—off on one of his trips. He hadn't told them where he was going this time, but he had seemed excited.

"Great! Let's get these home to Ma," said Penelope.

Back at the boardinghouse, Ma decided to open Charlie's letter first. She scanned the letter quickly, then shook her head and laughed.

"Well, Charlie warned us that he had a bad case of gold fever. Listen to this, children." She shared the letter, which was dated two weeks earlier.

Dear Tuckers,

Hello to you all! I have some big news, and I'll just go ahead and say it. I'm out in the gold fields! I just had to give it a try. I didn't tell you where I was going because I didn't want you to talk me out of it. I have not gone crazy, but—as you know—I have the "fever."

I expected to be home by now, but something wonderful has happened. I've found a promising site. In fact, I've already taken a good deal of gold from it.

Now I'm not sure when I will return. I plan to keep digging as long as the gold is there. Then I'll be on my way back to San Francisco. But only for

a while. I want to travel the world for a time.
Once I've made my fortune—no more hard work
for Charlie Simpson!

I know that you will continue to run the
boardinghouse in my absence. It's good to have
people there I can trust.

Fondly,
Charlie

Ma's hands shook as she put down the letter.

"What is it, Ma?" asked Penelope.

"Don't you think it's wonderful that Charlie's
struck it rich?" added Sam.

"Yes, it's wonderful," said Ma. "It's just . . ."

"What?" asked Penelope.

"I wonder what he'll decide to do with the
boardinghouse. If he sells it, we may be out of a
job—and out of a place to live."

"Oh," said Penelope in a low voice. "I hadn't
thought of that."

"Well, there's no point in worrying about trouble
that hasn't found us yet," said Ma. "Let's see what
Uncle James has to say."

"Maybe he struck it rich, too!" exclaimed Sam.
"Read his letter to us, will you, Pen?"

Penelope unfolded the letter and began reading.

Dear Family,

How is everyone? Are you still turning away boarders? Did you receive the gold flakes I sent last time? I know it wasn't much, but it's the best I could do. I am so sorry that I haven't written for a couple of weeks. It took me a while to save up for more writing paper.

I'm still working near Sutter's Fort with a few men from the Jackson Expedition. I'm considering moving on soon. This area is overrun with diggers, and every spot of land is spoken for. I'd like to try my luck someplace new — maybe a camp closer to San Francisco so I can visit more often.

Did I mention before that I ran into a Mr. Tuttle from Clinton, Iowa? I painted his portrait a couple of years ago. He was a wealthy farmer back then. It was strange working beside him in the field. He's not doing well. From what I have heard, he's lost a great deal of the fortune he already had by making reckless deals out here in gold country. When I saw him, all he could talk about was how much gold he had to find that week. I think he must be gambling — and losing. It's such a shame. Greed brought him out here, and now greed seems to be destroying him.

I work from first light to last every day. The

conditions are rough, and the pressure men feel to make a big "find" is huge. There's a lot at stake for many, especially the ones who promised their families back East (or in Russia, or Spain, or Chile) that they would return with lots of money.

I was robbed the other day. I'm told it won't be the last time! There's a lot of thieving out here. Some men make big scores one day, then have the gold stolen from them on their way back to their tents that same evening. You learn not to act excited when you make a good find. That only attracts the wrong kind of attention.

I miss you all very much. I hope to be able to visit soon, and to send more gold—I just need to find the right spot!

My love,
James

P.S. to Sam: No, gold isn't just lying on the ground, and we don't walk around shoveling it into our pockets! What have you been reading?

When Penelope finished, she said, "I wish Uncle James would come back to San Francisco. He could help us with the boardinghouse."

"Come back?" asked Sam. "Why would he do that? He's looking for gold!"

"I don't think he's ready to return, Penelope," said Ma. "James is a proud man, and he wants to make his own way."

"He *would* be making his own way if he worked here," said Penelope.

"But it wouldn't be enough for him, Penelope," Ma said. "Deciding to close the dry goods shop was hard on your uncle. He felt like he let your father—and us—down."

"That's silly!" said Penelope. "It wasn't his fault."

"We know that," said Ma, "but James feels bad about it anyway. He wants to succeed in California so he can feel like he is keeping his promise to your father."

The sound of the front door opening signaled the end of the conversation. A new boarder must have arrived.

Penelope stuck the letter in her pocket. "Well, I miss him," she sighed.

"Is that so?" asked a familiar voice. A tall, brown-haired man grinned at them from the doorway.

"Uncle James!" Penelope cried. She and Sam rushed into his open arms.

An Unexpected Bequest

"**H**ere's another piece of pie for you, Uncle James," said Penelope. "I saved it from supper." She put a plate on the table in front of her uncle. The dining room was empty now, except for the Tuckers. All the boarders had gone off to their rooms for the night, giving the family some privacy.

"Thank you," her uncle said. "I shouldn't eat another bite, but it's too good to turn down. Especially after what we've been eating out in the diggings!"

Penelope watched as he picked up his fork. It's so good to have him here for a visit, she thought. However, she was worried. Uncle James was even thinner than he had been. He seemed tired—and sad, too.

"Did you hear that we got a letter from Charlie?" Sam asked as his sister took a seat on the bench beside him.

The fork paused on its way to James's mouth. He put it down, then looked from Sam to Penelope to Ma. "What letter?"

"The one we got today—along with yours," Penelope replied.

"Charlie struck it rich, Uncle James!" exclaimed Sam. "Isn't that great news?"

"Yes," said her uncle. Penelope was confused by his lack of enthusiasm.

Now Ma joined in. "As you might guess, he isn't too interested in the boardinghouse anymore, James. He wants us to run it for now. So I am a bit worried about what the future holds for us. Though I certainly don't begrudge Charlie his gold," she hastened to add.

"Well," said James, "it seems that you're all doing a wonderful job running the house. I wouldn't worry." He hesitated, as if about to add something more. Then he looked at Penelope and Sam and his eyes dropped to his plate. He forked up a piece of pie and chewed thoughtfully.

"How long are you home for, James?" asked Ma. "We've really missed you."

"As a matter of fact," said Uncle James, "I have decided to leave the diggings. I was waiting for the right time to say so, and now seems as good as any."

"I'm glad," said Ma softly.

"So am I!" said Sam. "Though I still think you could've struck it rich."

Only Penelope remained silent. She was surprised at the angry thoughts racing through her mind. She had missed her uncle terribly and had wanted him back with the rest of the family. Still, she suddenly felt betrayed.

James continued. "I've seen a lot of tragedy in the fields, and I'm ready to get back to a normal life. I'm not sure what I'll do, but I'll figure something out."

Penelope couldn't hold back. "That's it?" she cried, jumping to her feet. "You're done with gold? You dragged us to this horrible place—and now we're stuck here for good? I can't believe it!"

"Penelope!" Ma said sternly. "I am shocked. You will *not* speak in that tone. Apologize at once."

Penelope already regretted her angry words. Taking a deep breath, she looked at her uncle. "I apologize, Uncle James. I had no call to say such things. And I really am glad to have you back."

James stood up and put his arms around his niece. Penelope welcomed his hug, but it didn't change how she felt. After all this, now it seemed that leaving home had been unnecessary.

"I wanted things to be different, Penelope," James said with a sigh. "I wanted to make it big in California. I'm sorry you don't like it here, but I think we can make a good life for ourselves."

"Charlie will have ideas about what kind of work you can do," Sam said. "He's full of plans."

At that, Uncle James let go of Penelope and sank into a chair. "Charlie is another reason I came back," he said heavily. "I'm afraid I have some sad news." He looked at Ma and added, "I was going to wait to tell you after the children had gone to bed. But they need to know, too."

"What is it, James?" Ma asked.

"Charlie's camp wasn't far from mine," he said. "So I soon heard that he was at the diggings. Then last week a man came with a message from Charlie."

Penelope felt a sudden chill, as if someone had left a window open. She hugged herself tightly as her uncle continued.

"As soon as I saw the man's face, I knew he bore bad news. It seems that cholera had swept through the camp. Many of the miners died— including Charlie."

Ma gasped and Sam's usual grin disappeared. A tear slid down Penelope's cheek. They knew all about cholera. They understood how Charlie must have suffered.

"Charlie had one last wish," James continued. "He explained it in a note to me. His gold was gone, the note said. He had been too weak to protect it from thieves. But he still had something of value left. And he wanted to be sure it was taken care of."

"The boardinghouse?" Ma whispered.

"Yes. He signed it over to the family," Uncle James replied. He looked into three sad faces and added, "*This* family, I mean. He said his cousin didn't need it. And that *you* had become his family. He wanted you to stay here and run the boardinghouse. Or do whatever you like with it."

There was silence as they all took in the news. Penelope was overwhelmed with sorrow at Charlie's death. And with amazement at his generosity.

At last Ma spoke. "Oh, James," she said, "this is too much. I can't believe Charlie is gone. He was our friend. He helped us stay together. We already owed him a giant debt. I don't know what to do."

"You don't have to do anything yet," said Uncle James. "Later you can talk with Charlie's lawyer and decide what's right for the family."

Uncle James looked at Penelope and said, "Perhaps you won't even want to stay in San Francisco. Selling this house would net enough money to go back East."

"Go back East!" cried Sam. "We wouldn't do that, would we, Ma?"

"Hush, Sam," said Ma. "There's no cause to talk about that now. Right now we just need to mourn Charlie." Then she looked at James. "And don't forget that you belong to this family, too. You'll be part of whatever decision we make."

The four of them sat for another hour. They talked about Charlie and his many kindnesses. Then, as the darkness deepened, James told about his own experiences as a miner.

"It's a hard life," he said. "Most days I spent a good ten hours standing in ice-cold water up to my knees. I'd dig, sift, and wash—and end up with a few flecks of gold in my pan. Then I had to do it all again. Gold is getting harder to find, and the miners are becoming less friendly to each other every day."

"You did the right thing by coming back, Uncle James," said Penelope. She wanted to erase the memory of her earlier outburst. "We've had all sorts of boarders who've done the same thing."

"Eventually you realize that the dream of a fortune isn't worth the risks you have to take," admitted James. "And now, I think I've talked long enough. It's time you children got to bed."

Over the next few days, Uncle James learned his way around San Francisco. At the same time, he looked for a job. While he knew he could be useful at the boardinghouse, he wanted to do more.

"Buck said he could use a clerk in the shoe store," James said one afternoon when he returned.

Penelope couldn't picture her uncle selling shoes.

Surely that wouldn't be any better a fit than selling dry goods had been. She was relieved when her mother protested.

"Please, James," Ma said. "You need to think things through. It's a big decision, and putting it off a week or two won't hurt."

Uncle James sighed. "You're right," he said. "I need to clear my head and figure out my next move. I've put this family through too many big changes already. I have to feel good about the next step. I owe it to you—and to myself."

His favorite head-clearing activity had always been painting, so Uncle James bought a few supplies. Soon the back parlor had become an artist's studio.

Penelope peeked in one evening while her uncle worked. He stopped painting when he noticed her.

"I'm sorry, Uncle James. Please don't stop," she said. "I didn't mean to disturb you. I just wanted to see what you're working on."

"Oh, it's really nothing, Penelope," Uncle James said. "Just a neighborhood scene."

Penelope stepped up to see the canvas. "That's Portsmouth Square!" she exclaimed. "It's wonderful! I feel like I'm standing right out on the street!"

"Thank you," James said. "That's the idea. It's nice when people feel what you intend them to feel."

"Are you going to sell it?" Penelope asked. She looked around at several other canvases leaning against the walls. Most of them were vivid depictions of life in San Francisco or on the Oregon-California trail. "You could sell these, too."

"No, no," he said. "I'm just fiddling around. I don't suppose anyone would want to buy these paintings."

"I would," said Penelope. "I'll bet others would,

too, and I'm not saying that because you're my uncle. They are really good, Uncle James. I wish I could paint. But I just don't have the talent for it!"

"Everybody's good at something," Uncle James assured her. "We can't all paint—just like we can't all find fortunes in gold." He picked up a brush, obviously eager to get back to work.

"I should get out of your way," Penelope said. Her uncle hardly noticed her leave.

Uncle James seems so content, Penelope thought as she walked off. More so than I have seen him since before Pa died. It would be nice if he could paint all the time, like he used to do.

And why not? she wondered. Surely I can do something to make that happen!

Trouble on Kearny Street!

Penelope headed downstairs to the kitchen before dawn. It was her turn to start breakfast for the boarders. She splashed water on her face to try to wake up. Then, yawning, she began cracking eggs into a large bowl.

Despite the early hour, Penelope's mind was busy. She was still thinking about how to make it possible for Uncle James to keep painting.

A half hour later, Ma and Sam joined her. Soon breakfast for a crowd took shape: coffee, scrambled eggs, bacon, potatoes, apple fritters, biscuits, and sausage gravy.

At last, Sam said, "It's time to bang the gong. Should I do it, Pen?"

"No, thanks," said Penelope. "I can take care of it."

As she lifted the mallet, someone pounded at the back door. Penelope looked at Ma, but before either of them could move, the door burst open. It was a neighbor.

"Fire!" he shouted. "There's a big fire on Kearny Street!"

"Where?" asked Uncle James, who had just entered the room. "And how fast is it moving?"

Feelings of dread filled Penelope as she heard the response. "It's just up the road, Mr. Tucker. It started at Dennison's Exchange. It's moving fast, too—spreading in both directions. One man's already dead from trying to stop it! There's talk that it could take the whole city!"

James grabbed his hat and said, "I'll go see what I can do. Sam, rouse the men upstairs. We'll need their help."

The door slammed shut behind Uncle James and the neighbor. From outside, Penelope could hear cries of "Fire! Fire!" ringing through the air.

Quickly, the boarders flew down the stairs and out to the street. There was no time to waste.

"Ma, will the fire spread all the way here?" Sam asked.

"Let's hope not," Ma replied. "Still, we should get out of the house, children. These wooden buildings go up quickly."

Untying her apron, she said to Penelope, "Please get the copy of *Pilgrim's Progress* from the parlor. I am not leaving it here to burn."

Trembling, Penelope ran into the parlor. She

knew exactly where to find the book. It had belonged to her father, and it was one of the only "frivolous" things Ma had brought with her from Independence.

Returning to the kitchen, Penelope found her mother and brother ready to go. She grabbed her cloak and they hurried through the back door.

Outside, yellow-orange flames shot up into the early morning sky. The air was filled with thick, black smoke. White ash fell like heated rain. It seemed as if the entire city was ablaze. The flimsy wood-framed buildings and canvas tents burned like dried tumbleweeds.

A bucket brigade formed on Kearny Street with Uncle James as its leader. Penelope, Sam, and Ma took their places. They passed bucket after bucket of water toward the fire. The smoke made it hard to see—and even harder to breathe. Ma and Penelope tied their bonnets around their mouths and noses. Sam tied a handkerchief around his. Ash and debris flew everywhere, and soon their hands and faces were a sooty mess.

If only San Francisco had a fire department, thought Penelope. But none had been organized yet. The city was too new.

The fire continued to creep closer and closer to the boardinghouse. They needed more water—

faster. As it was, there was no way to completely douse the angry flames. They could slow the inferno, but they couldn't stop it.

Then, with the people at the brink of exhaustion, an official gave an order. He directed the crowd to start pulling down buildings. If they couldn't stop the fire, they would destroy its fuel!

Uncle James and Sam joined the demolition crew, while Ma and Penelope stayed with the brigade. In horrified fascination, they watched as men used ropes to pull down the building five doors away from the boardinghouse. Then the one four doors away. Then three, then two . . .

Tears welled up in Penelope's eyes—and not just from the smoke. Faced with the loss of the boardinghouse, she suddenly realized how much it meant to her. It couldn't burn!

Then the demolition crew stopped. The fire was out! Portsmouth Square and an entire block of Kearny Street were gone. But the city was safe. And with one sad exception, so were its people.

The crowd erupted in cheers and hugs. Penelope threw her arms around her mother. "Oh, Ma," she said, "I was so scared."

"So was I, Penelope," said Ma in a shaky voice. "But we're all right. And so is our house."

Sam and Uncle James approached, their faces black with smoke. Together, they went into the boardinghouse.

Inside, it was clear that the smoke had done considerable damage. Still, things could have been so much worse.

Uncle James moved directly to the back parlor. Penelope followed. She knew he was checking on his paintings.

Most were soot-covered, even some that had been stacked behind other paintings. "Here's the one you liked so much, Penelope. The painting of Portsmouth Square," Uncle James said sadly. He was looking at a large canvas. The vivid colors were now dulled by soot.

The sight of the damaged painting made Penelope feel ill. The square had been beautiful—and now . . .

"It's gone," she said sadly.

Penelope was surprised at the depth of her feelings. Today she had seen the beauty and promise of a new city—*her* city—almost go up in flames. She had felt her neighbors' pain at losing their homes. And she had fought hard to save her own.

I guess this place has grown on me, she thought incredulously.

"The people are still here, Penelope. We'll rebuild what was lost," said Uncle James.

"I hope so," murmured Penelope. And she realized how much she wanted to help make that happen.

A Job for Uncle James

The next few days were a frenzy of activity. The Tuckers—along with others who had been spared—did all they could to ease the fire victims' burdens. They offered beds, clothing, food, and helping hands. The boardinghouse became a temporary shelter to scores of people whose homes had been swallowed by the fire. Every room had been filled. Some men even bedded down on the parlor floor for a few nights.

But now things were beginning to get back to normal. Those who had lost their homes had found new lodgings—several of them at Simpson's Boardinghouse. So there was more than enough work to keep Penelope busy.

"That's it," she said with satisfaction, placing the last dish in the cupboard. She was the only one helping Ma tonight, as Sam was running an errand.

"Thank you, dear," said Ma. "Why don't we go out in the parlor now. I know you enjoy listening to Uncle James and the others."

Penelope gave her mother a grateful smile. It was fun having so many people in the house. The parlor was always full. And someone was always talking about something interesting. Whether traveler or miner, every visitor had exciting experiences to share. Penelope didn't want to miss anything.

It wasn't only the boarders who filled the parlor. Friends like Buck and Rusty stopped by often for the company or to eat supper with the boarders. Jing-Li and her family came whenever they could spare time from their work. And many of the Tuckers' friends had become loyal customers of the Sun and Moon Chinese Eating Place.

This neighborhood is like an enormous family, Penelope thought as she entered the room. A bearded man was just winding down his tale of sailing around South America on his way out West. Then someone said, "What about you, James? What did you do before catching the fever?"

Uncle James laughed. "Well, folks, as some of you know, I was a painter. I traveled all over Iowa, Missouri, and Arkansas. And I painted just about anything people asked me to."

"Including fences?" asked one fellow with a grin.

"Well, I didn't have to do that," said James. He went on to tell a story of painting a family portrait that included three chickens and a milk cow. "The animals were part of the family," he said. "So they were part of the painting. Believe me, it's hard to get a chicken to sit still for its portrait."

"It's also hard to know whether to believe you or not," commented one man. James smiled, but said nothing to confirm or deny his story.

"Uncle James is a *real* artist," Penelope announced before anyone could launch into another long tale. "Would you like to see his work?"

"I sure would, Miss Penelope," said the bearded man.

"So would I," said Rusty. Several others agreed.

Uncle James quieted the rush of voices. "It's bad enough that they have to listen to my stories, Penelope. Let's not bore them further by making them look at my paintings. Besides, folks, most of my canvases were damaged by the smoke. Now, who's brave enough to challenge me to a game of checkers?"

"Nice try, James," said Buck. "We want to see your paintings!"

The others egged Uncle James on until he gave in. "Penelope," he said, "since you started all this, I'll let you go select something."

Penelope hurried into the back parlor and brought out her favorite painting—the one of Portsmouth Square. Uncle James had cleaned it up as best he could. Now Penelope held the canvas so everyone could see.

"What do you think?" she asked. "Isn't it terrific?"

"It looks like you captured the smoke perfectly, James," said Buck. "Why, I can almost smell it!"

"Hey, Buck," someone called out, "stop your kidding."

Buck turned to James. "I *was* joking, you know. But even with the smoke damage, it's easy to see that you do fine work."

"I had no idea I knew a true artist," said Rusty. "That scene is so real that it about breaks my heart to see it."

"Mine, too," said an older man. "Would you consider selling the painting to me, James? I'd give you twenty dollars for it."

"And what else can you show us?" asked Buck.

Before Uncle James could protest, Penelope gestured toward the door that led to the back parlor. "This way to the James Tucker Art Studio," she said.

Soon offers were flying. "I love this portrait of Penelope and Sam," one boarder said. He pulled a folded paper from his pocket and unwrapped a faded image of a little girl. "Could you use this to do a portrait of my daughter?"

"I'll give you twenty-five dollars for this map of

the Oregon-California Trail," said Buck. "I know at least a dozen people who'd pay the same for one."

James was clearly stunned. But Penelope could tell that he was also happy. So was she. She felt she'd had a hand in making something special happen.

Buck slapped Uncle James on the back. "I know you've been looking for work. Seems to me that you could make a nice living here as an artist."

"Don't get carried away, Buck," said Uncle James. "People here are friends and neighbors. There's no guarantee my work would get the same reception from strangers."

"I thought you did this for a living once before," said Rusty. "What's different now?"

James shook his head. "I was a different man when I worked as a traveling artist," he said. "I didn't have any roots, and I didn't have much responsibility. I don't want to go back to that life."

"Who says you have to be a *traveling* artist, James?" asked Ma. "You can paint right here, as you have been doing. You just need to look at it as a job, not something you 'fiddle around' with."

"Oh, Uncle James!" said Penelope. "Ma's right. Please set up a studio here. I know that Pa would want you to. I can't think of anything better!"

Uncle James laughed. "You can't, can you?" He looked around at all the smiling faces. He said, "Well, I am a '49er, and we '49ers are bound to try and try, and then try some more!"

"Here, here!" shouted Rusty. Then Buck broke into a chorus of "The Days of '49." Everyone joined in—

My comrades they all loved me well,
A jolly saucy crew.
A few hard cases I will recall
Though they all were brave and true.
Whatever the pinch they never would flinch,
They never would fret or whine.
Like good old bricks they stood the kicks
In the days of '49.

The Rush Is Over

Penelope answered the front door. It was Mr. Wilcox, one of Uncle James's best customers. In the two months that Uncle James had been painting full-time, Mr. Wilcox had ordered three portraits!

"Hello, Penelope. Is your uncle in?"

"He's been waiting for you, Mr. Wilcox," Penelope said.

As she finished speaking, Uncle James walked through the door that led into his studio. He carried a framed portrait. "Mr. Wilcox," he said, "your picture is ready."

Mr. Wilcox studied his portrait for a moment, then broke into a wide grin. His smile showed two front teeth of gold, and several holes where teeth were missing.

"It's a perfect likeness, James," he said. "That's what I like best about your work. You are so precise, so *accurate*. I'll be back next month for my wife's portrait. I trust it will be a stunning representation of her beauty."

"Of course. I will see you next month, sir," said Uncle James.

As soon as the door closed behind Mr. Wilcox, Penelope dissolved into giggles.

"What's so funny?" Uncle James asked with a straight face.

"Mr. Wilcox thinks that you're *accurate!*" Penelope laughed. "No wonder he keeps coming back—you showed him with a full smile!"

"Yes?" Uncle James pretended not to know what she was hinting at.

"Uncle James," Penelope half-scolded. "You painted him with a mouth full of real teeth. Not to mention that you scaled down his ears. The portrait looks almost nothing like him!"

"That's where you are wrong, my dear," said Uncle James. "It looks exactly like how Mr. Wilcox pictures himself. And remember, he is a paying customer. People like him are my bread and butter."

"You mean they're your *gold*, don't you, Uncle James?" Penelope offered.

Uncle James nodded slowly. "Yes, I suppose that *is* what I mean. Penelope, you've given me an excellent idea."

He disappeared for the rest of the afternoon. When he emerged from his studio, he carried something under one arm. "Where is everybody?"

he called. "I have something to show you."

"In here," a voice said from the kitchen, where Penelope, Sam, and Ma were getting things set up for supper.

"Is that a painting, Uncle James?" asked Penelope as he entered the room.

"It certainly is," he replied. He turned to Ma and said, "I know that you've been trying to decide on a new name for the boardinghouse. I thought of one, and I think you'll approve. Penelope gave me the idea."

"What is it?" asked Ma.

"Well," Uncle James said, pausing dramatically, "it's a name that carries a lot of meaning for us. We came to California chasing a dream. A dream of wealth and happiness.

"Like many others, we learned that true happiness has nothing to do with wealth—and a lot to do with family. We found ourselves coming full circle—back to doing the kind of work we were meant to do. And living the kind of life we were meant to live.

"I think we would all agree that the streets of this community *are* paved with gold. It might not be the kind of gold we were looking for, but it's the kind of gold we need."

Penelope simply could not wait any longer.

"Have you finished your speech yet, Uncle James?"

"Penelope," said Ma firmly, "let your uncle continue."

"No," said Uncle James, "Penelope is right. I have gone on long enough. I think it's time for the official presentation. Ready, everyone?"

Sam answered for them all with his version of an imaginary trumpet call.

With a great flourish, Uncle James turned the board around. It was a sign. At one side, he had painted a majestic elephant. The beast's trunk pointed to elegant lettering.

"Tuckers' Gold!" exclaimed Penelope. "That's a wonderful idea!"

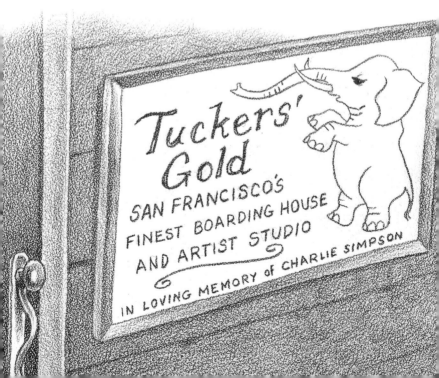

"Let's hang the sign outside now!" shouted Sam.

"Yes," said Ma. "It's a perfect name, James."

The whole family trooped outside. Penelope watched as Uncle James and Sam nailed the sign to the front of the house, next to the door.

She could hardly believe that less than six months ago she had wanted to leave San Francisco. Think of all the things I would have missed, she marveled: fighting a terrible fire, helping to build a new city, meeting people from all over the world . . .

We truly did find our gold, she thought. Tuckers' gold.

A Snapshot of San Francisco
The California Gold Rush (1846—1849)

January 30, 1847 Yerba Buena (meaning "the place of good grass") was renamed San Francisco.

April 19, 1847 Twice-weekly horseback mail service began between San Francisco and San Diego.

January 24, 1848 James Marshall discovered gold at Sutter's Mill.

February 2, 1848 California became part of the United States after the Mexican War ended.

March 15, 1848 The *Californian* reported the discovery of gold at Sutter's Mill. The news was not widely believed in San Francisco.

March 25, 1848 The *California Star* reported the discovery of gold. Still little attention was paid.

April 1, 1848 The *California Star* also published a special edition called the "Prospects of California." Extra copies were printed and sent East.

May 12, 1848 Sam Brannan officially started "gold fever" in San Francisco when he waved a bottle of gold dust. Men rushed to the fields.

106

May 29, 1848 The *Californian* reported, "The whole country from San Francisco to Los Angeles, and from the seashore to the base of the Sierra Nevadas, resounds with the sordid cry of GOLD, GOLD, GOLD! while the field is left half-planted, the house half-built, and everything neglected but the manufacture of shovels and pickaxes." The story contained the first published mention of the phrase that became so well-known. It said that in the "rush for gold," it was every man for himself.

June 10, 1848 The *California Star* reported that towns emptied as people rushed to the gold fields. Within four days, the newspaper shut down.

September 10, 1848 The price of gold dust was set at sixteen dollars per ounce.

November 18, 1848 Edward Cleveland Kemble resumed publishing the *Star and Californian*—a new newspaper that was a combination of the *California Star* and the *Californian.*

December 5, 1848 President Polk confirmed the discovery of gold in California.

January 22, 1849 The *Alta California* became the first daily newspaper in California.

April 1849 Wagon trains began departing from St. Joseph, Missouri, on a 2,000-mile overland journey to California.

August 7, 1849 Wright and Co. of San Francisco asked Governor Riley for permission to mint five-dollar and ten-dollar gold coins to relieve the money shortage.

November 10, 1849 The Collector of the Port reported that 697 ships had arrived since April 1; 401 were American, 296 were foreign.

December 24, 1849 The first Great Fire destroyed most of the city.

December 25, 1849 Frederick D. Kohler and David C. Broderick organized a fire department for San Francisco.

December 28, 1849 Edward Otis organized the Independent Unpaid Axe Volunteer Fire Company.

December 31, 1849 San Francisco's population was estimated at 100,000. About 35,000 people had come by sea, 3,000 sailors had deserted their ships, and 42,000 people had come overland.